THE PRINCIPAL'S NEW CLOTHES

by Stephanie Calmenson

illustrated by Denise Brunkus

Scholastic Inc.
New York   Toronto   London   Auckland   Sydney

ISBN 0-590-44778-5

12 11 10 9 8 7 6   3 4 5 6/9

Printed in the U.S.A.   08

To Eva
—S.C.

For my associates,
Wayne and
Kate the
Great
—D.B.

Mr. Bundy is the principal of P.S. 88.
He is also the sharpest dresser in town.

His students never miss a day of school.
They like to see what he is wearing.
"Looking good, Mr. B!" they always say.

Mr. Bundy has so many clothes,
he can go a whole month
and not wear the same suit twice.
Sometimes he changes at lunchtime,
just to show off.

One day a man and a woman,
who said they were tailors,
called on Mr. Bundy.
Their card said,

MOE AND IVY
WE MAKE SUITS THAT SUIT YOU FINE

But they were not really tailors.
They were tricksters.

"Greetings, Mr. B," said Ivy.
"How would you like to buy
an amazing, one-of-a-kind suit?"

"I have so many suits already,"
said Mr. Bundy.

"Ah, but this is no ordinary suit,"
said Moe. "It has special powers."

"What do you mean?" asked Mr. Bundy.

Moe looked to his left.
He looked to his right.
Then he whispered in Mr. Bundy's ear,
"We make our clothes from special cloth.
It is invisible to anyone who is
no good at his job or just plain stupid."

"Really?" said Mr. Bundy.

"Yes," said Ivy.
"Not only will you look great, but
 you can find out if anyone in your school
 is no good at his job or stupid."

"That *is* amazing!" cried Mr. Bundy.

"Now if you'll take off your jacket
 and lift up your arms, sir,"
said Ivy, grinning,
"we will take your measurements."

"We will also take your money," mumbled Moe.

The next day, Moe and Ivy
set up a workshop in the gym.
It was not long before the whole school
heard about the amazing cloth
and wanted to see it.
Students asked to be excused
to get a drink of water.
Then they ran to the gym to peek.
Teachers said they were
going next door to borrow chalk.
Then they ran to the gym, too,
but no one could see a thing.

By the end of the week,
Mr. Bundy began to wonder
what his new clothes looked like.
But he was also a little worried.
What if he could not see the cloth?
So he sent his vice principal,
Ms. Moore, to have a look.
Ms. Moore was smart
and good at her job.
She would have no trouble
seeing the special cloth.

Ms. Moore hurried to the gym.
She knocked on the door.
"Mr. Bundy sent me
to see his new clothes,"
she called over the noise
of the whirring machines.
A moment later the door
opened a crack and
Ms. Moore slipped inside.

"What do you think?" asked Moe.
"Have you ever seen anything like it?"

Poor Ms. Moore!
She could not see a thing.
"Can it be that I am stupid,
or unfit for my job?" she wondered.
"I've tried so hard
to be a good vice principal."

She took off her glasses,
wiped them, and looked again.
But it was no use.
Ms. Moore had to think fast.
If she told the truth,
she might get fired.
"It's…it's beautiful!" she said.
"I'm going to tell Mr. Bundy right now
how much I like his new clothes."

"Your suit is great!"
Ms. Moore told Mr. Bundy.
"I've never seen anything like it!
And now I've got to run and
make a phone call. 'Bye!"
She hurried off before Mr. Bundy
could ask any questions.

Now Mr. Bundy was more curious than ever.

He stopped Roger in the hall.
Roger was one of the smartest
students in the school.
If he couldn't see the suit, nobody could.
"Say, Roger," said Mr. Bundy,
"do me a favor and find out
how my new suit is coming along."

Roger couldn't believe his ears.
"Wow!" he said.
"I'll be the first one to see
the principal's new clothes!
Wait till the class hears about this!"
And he raced off to the gym.

The door was still open,
so Roger peeked inside.
He could see Moe and Ivy
at their sewing machines,
hard at work.
But he could not see the cloth!
"Oh, no!" Roger thought.
"If Mrs. Feeney finds out
I can't see this cloth,
she'll say I'm stupid.
She'll fail me for sure."

On the way back to his class,
Roger poked his head
into Mr. Bundy's office.
"Super suit!" he said.

"What does it look like?"
asked Mr. Bundy.

"I can't stop now, Mr. B.
Mrs. Feeney is giving a test,
and I wouldn't want to miss it."

Mr. Bundy couldn't stand it any longer.
"I'll have to go see for myself."
He marched down the hall
and walked into the gym.

Mr. Bundy looked at the empty machines.
He blinked once. He blinked twice.
He began to tremble.

"How can this be?" he wondered.
"Am I really no good at my job?"

"Is there anything wrong?" asked Ivy.

"Oh, no!" said Mr. Bundy.
"The suit is…it's…
well…it's…fantastic!
I can hardly wait to try it on."

Mr. Bundy handed Moe and Ivy
two gold stars to show how much
he liked his new suit.
"I'd like to wear the suit
to the assembly tomorrow," he said.
"But I guess it won't be ready...."
He turned to go.

"Yes, it will!" said Moe.
"We will work on it all night
and bring it to your house
in the morning."

That night, Mr. Bundy
dreamed cold and drafty dreams.

Early the next morning
Moe and Ivy appeared,
holding their empty hangers
in the air.

Ivy waited in the other room
while Moe helped Mr. Bundy
put on his new clothes.
"You must be careful stepping
into the pants," he said.
"This cloth is very delicate."

Ivy tried not to look at Mr. Bundy.
"Aren't your new clothes light?" she asked.
"It's almost like having
nothing on at all, isn't it?"
Mr. Bundy stared at himself in the mirror.
He prayed that the rest of the world
was smarter and fitter than he.

"Are you coming to the assembly?"
asked Mr. Bundy.

"Thanks, but no thanks," said Ivy.
"We have a bus to catch.
And now, if you could pay us, we'll just run along."

Moe handed Mr. Bundy the bill.
Mr. Bundy handed Moe
a great deal of money.

On the way to school,
Mr. Bundy's neighbors all raved
about the clothes they did not see.
After all, they did not want
their friends to find out that
they were stupid or no good at their jobs.

Mr. Bundy walked into the auditorium.
As he walked down the aisle,
he could hear whispers all around him.
Mr. Bundy thought he must be the
only stupid person in town.

Suddenly a kindergarten child called out,
"The principal's in his underwear!"
That did it! Everyone burst out laughing.
The truth had been told.
Mr. Bundy and the teachers and students
knew they had been tricked.
No one had been willing
to tell the truth because
they were worried about
what others would think of them.
Mr. Bundy stood on stage, red in the face,
knees shaking from the chill.
But not for long.

The kids and teachers
wanted to help Mr. Bundy.
They began passing up
shirts and sweatpants,
jackets and ties and caps.
Soon Mr. Bundy had a new suit.

"Looking good, Mr. B!" called Roger from the back row.

Mr. Bundy called the kindergarten child
up onto the stage.
He shook her hand and gave her a gold star.
"Thank you for telling the truth, Alice," he said.

Everyone cheered. They knew Mr. Bundy
was smart and good at his job. And they all agreed...

Mr. Bundy was still the sharpest dresser in town.